The Official

Disney

ZOOTOPIA

HANDBOOK

randomhousekids.com

ISBN 978-0-7364-3395-2

Printed in the United States of America

10 9 8 7 6 5 4 3 2 1

The Official

ZOOTOPIA

HANDBOOK

Your guide to the city!

By
**Suzanne
Francis**

Random House 🏠 New York

WELCOME
TO ZOOTOPIA

Whenever I find myself in the modern metropolis of Zootopia, I discover a new reason to love it. From the tops of its towering skyscrapers to the depths of its subway system, Zootopia pulses with a fur-bristling energy.

Animals from every environment live together in this mammal melting pot—a place where no matter who you are, the biggest giraffe or the smallest shrew, you can be anything you want to be. It also has millions of things to eat, see, and do.

Let the Official Zootopia Handbook be your guide to this incredible city and its diverse boroughs. — **Goldie**

downtown

Tundratown

sahara square

st

s

the canals

Goldie Gnu: Editor in Chief

ZOOTOPIA:
THE LAND OF EVERY BODY

Whether you're moving here for good or just swinging by for a visit, there's a place for you in Zootopia. The city's uniquely designed living spaces suit animals of all sizes, so no one feels out of place. Thanks to thoughtful planning, every body can live, work, and play together in harmony.

Homes are built to accommodate every kind of body.

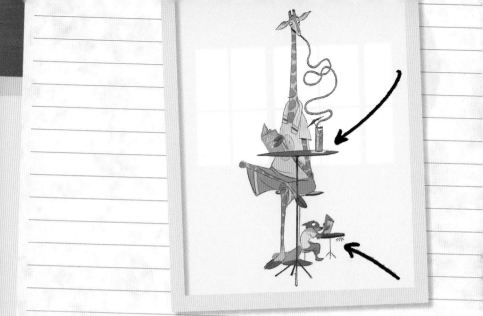

Seating arrangements at cafés are maximized by having tables under tables. Watch out for falling crumbs!

And in some workplaces, desks of animals of different sizes are nestled up close to one another.

THE ANIMALS OF ZOOTOPIA

Zootopia is home to the widest variety of mammals in the world. Predator and prey alike shop, eat, and work together in harmony. Here, animals have the opportunity to choose their careers. In Zootopia, anyone can be anything, so the sky's the limit!

From the biggest lion to the smallest mouse, everyone is welcome in Zootopia!

THE ZOOTOPIA EXPERIENCE

Visit the Rainforest District. Sahara Square. Tundratown. Little Rodentia. And even the suburb, Bunnyburrow! This guide will take you through each section of Zootopia, highlighting must-see sights, restaurants, local favorites, and more.

Replace with updated map.

steam

Enormous tree-like pipe systems pump up the water and release it as steam and rain at the top

overgrown

roads and balconies

water

SAVANNAH CENTRAL:
The main plaza in town (probably built around the original watering hole - now a Bellagio style fountain) features a trainstation, the police building, City Hall (with Lionheart - the mayor's office)

CENTRAL STATION

POLICE BUILDING

BURROW BURROUGHS
POPULATION

BURROW BORROUGH

Hopps Family Home

Deep overgrown valleys towards downtown. Lots of small islands and waterways on the outside

RAINFOREST DISTRICT

Hopps and Nick will investigate in the Rainforest.

rainbow

european inspired architecture

trainstation

SAVANNAH CENTRAL
(central plaza)

Hopps meter maid cart

THE WATERHOLE
(a stadium - plays no role anymore)

bridge

MOUNTAINS
(TUNNEL)

The skyscrapers of Downtown are built on the highest point of Zootopia

DOWNTOWN

animal features

variety of scales

city hall fountain

police building

LITTLE RODENTIA

pine forrest
mountain range surround Tundratown on the far side snowy pines on the border

Gondolas

TUNDRATOWN
rises up towards Downtown

CLIMATE W

african inspired buildings

SAHARA SQUARE

Burrow Borrough Train Station

Train to Zootopia   Zootopia's districts are connected with a monorail system

Inside, You'll Find:

Greatest Grub:
All the best restaurants for grazing, gorging, and nibbling.

Zootopians to Watch:
Profiles and interviews with some of Zootopia's most interesting residents.

Rip-Roarin' Nights:
The top nighttime haunts for nocturnal party mammals.

Local Faves:
Residents give you the lowdown on their favorite spots.

Travel Tips:
Handy tricks and tips for the traveling mammal.

Savanna Central is in the middle of downtown Zootopia. There you'll find Central Station, City Hall, and the Zootopia Police Department.

THE RAINFOREST DISTRICT

The Rainforest District is as lush, green, and beautiful as it is intriguing. With its constant mist, the air stays warm, humid, and wet—just the way those who live here like it.

Whether you explore the rainforest by car, on foot, by boat, or from high above the treetops in a gondola, you're in for a treat.

retreat to the scenic
Rainforest
district

ZOOTOPIA

Like a gentle spring shower, the mist of the Rainforest District is nourishing and refreshing. The weather here keeps fur and skin healthy and moisturized.

But animals who prefer to stay dry won't seem out of place carrying brightly colored umbrellas—especially when the steam trees let loose with one of their frequent downpours!

Travel Tip:
All wet?
Don't get upset!
Bring an umbrella!

Fashion and functionality have a price. Umbrellas sell for top dollar around attractions in the area—so be sure to bring one along!

Don't miss the incredible waterfalls—the Rainforest District is home to some of the tallest falls in the world.

Some of the rainforest's most beautiful homes are located high in the treetops. And a ride on the gondola can give you a view of those homes.

LOCAL FAVE:
MISTY'S ON THE VINE

Misty's has been serving the Rainforest District for over 45 years. Open 24 hours a day, it's rated one of the top places for buggy burgers in the city.

"Don't leave the canopy without sinking your fangs into Misty's Bug Burger. It's the buggiest in town!"

– Mel B.

LITTLE RODENTIA

Nestled in downtown Zootopia, this neat and tidy gated community is home to Zootopia's smallest residents—mice, gerbils, rats, and other small rodents. There is a height requirement to enter so residents remain safe from potential stomping incidents. Those who are too tall to enter can still enjoy a glimpse of this quaint community from outside its gates.

THE BIG DONUT
O-M-Goodness!

Ads

Mighty Roar for Another FOUR!

Let's Do This! Reelect Mayor Lionheart!

Little Rodentia's Main Street is lined with brownstones and popular restaurants like Clark's Leafy Greens, Chez Cheez, and other quirky shops, such as Albert's Paw Readings.

Residents like Marge Pellet can do all their shopping on Main Street. "Clark's has the freshest fruits and vegetables around. I just can't scurry by without stopping for a nibble."

LITTLE RODENTIA RESTAURATEUR CHARLES CHEEZ III

Charles Cheez III, owner of the constantly packed Chez Cheez (and Chez Cheez warehouse), talks to the Official Zootopia Handbook about his popular family restaurant.

OZH: How would you describe Chez Cheez?

CC: I'll do it in three words, and they all start with the letter F: Fun. Family. Food.

OZH: What is your favorite dish?

CC: I've been eating a cheese-galore Squeaky Meal at least once a week since I was a tot and still love it. It's fun.

OZH: Your cheesecake is famous. What's your secret?

CC: *(laughs)* I'll never tell. The ghost of my great-great-grandfather would kick my rump if I answered that question. Go get yourself a slice.

BUNNYBURROW

Outside the city of Zootopia are miles and miles of rolling green hills and farmland. Bunnies call quaint Bunnyburrow home and live in charming houses built into the countryside. There is currently a population boom that shows no sign of slowing down.

A family posing for a picture in Bunnyburrow. But with 276 kids, it's hard to get everyone in one shot.

LOCAL FAVE:
CARROT DAYS FESTIVAL

Visit Bunnyburrow during the Carrot Days Festival to get a full dose of local flavor. Talent contests, food booths, games, and rides make this great fun for the whole family. Of course, you'll also enjoy lots and lots of that deliciously crunchy orange veggie!

No car? No problem. Hit Bunnyburrow via Rabbit Transit. Trains depart from Central Station, in downtown Zootopia, every hour on the hour, from 7 a.m. until 8 p.m.

GREAT GETAWAYS ON RABBIT TRANSIT!

Save money and time, and relax.
Hop aboard the Bunny Train.
Join our frequent-rider program and earn points toward free rides!

FREE WIRELESS!

Ad

Sponsored by the Rabbit Transit Authority

They are teen friendly!
"Rabbit Transit is totally twitchin'!"

— Penny, age 14

Put quote on ad to attract younger audience.

TUNDRATOWN

Tundratown glistens with snow and ice all year long and is kept frigid thanks to its climate-controlling wall. Polar bears, wolves, moose, yaks, reindeer, and other cold-loving animals make this neighborhood their home, but anyone can visit any time they start yearning to ice skate or throw a snowball.

A feat of engineering, the climate wall that separates the boroughs of Tundratown and Sahara Square keeps Tundratown a wintery wonderland while blowing hot air on Sahara Square, keeping it dry and toasty warm. Tours of the facilities are available. We recommend that you call ahead to book tours for large groups and herds.

For fashionistas, there is no better shopping than in the Fashion District.

Hit the stores between 8 and 10 a.m. on Saturdays.

Hunt for deals during Morning Madness. (Not for the meek: be prepared to paw your way through the crowds!)

LOCAL FAVE:
THE THAW

Thaw
picture
to come

The Thaw offers live music and dancing in an upscale atmosphere. Our plunging pool is always just above freezing!

"When you're in the mood to chill, hit up The Thaw on Friday nights for live music, food, and an after-dinner plunge. It's cooler than cool."
–Ivan Petrovovovid

The itching is driving me crazy!

SAHARA
SQUARE

Soak up the sun in Sahara Square. This toasty section of Zootopia has sand, sun, and fun—all day and all night.

Three-time boogie board champion Stone Kole can often be seen practicing along the Sahara coast. "Dude, the Sahara coast is always cranking. They're always coming at me, like 'Raaahh,' and I'm amped in the pit. And then I'm like 'Boom, boom, boom! Shaaaaaah!' They're the most awesome-possum waves in Zootopia. Paws down, dude. Paws down."

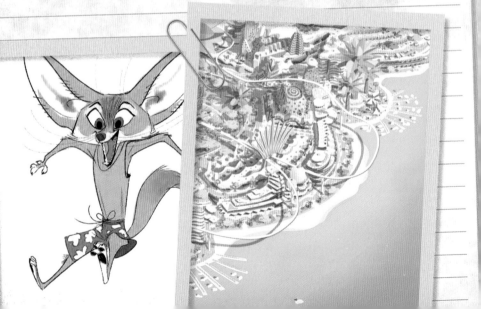

LOCAL FAVE:
SUNDAY MEERKAT MARKET

Every Sunday the open-air market in Sahara Square comes alive with dazzling sights, sounds, and smells. Enjoy live music, browse locally made wares, or grab a bite to eat.

There's more than one reason to go to the market. These otters met there 20 years ago and are still together.

"Years ago I saw a young lady sampling spicy lentils at the Sunday Meerkat Market." —Mr. Otterton

"And I saw a young man watching me eat spicy lentils." —Mrs. Otterton

"I went for lunch." —Mr. Otterton

"I didn't buy the lentils." —Mrs. Otterton

"We both found love." —Mr. and Mrs. Otterton

LOCAL FAVE:
MYSTIC SPRING OASIS

Mammals of all shapes and sizes flock to the Mystic Spring Oasis to relax, rewind, reset, and return to the basics.

Enjoy the spa, take a yoga class, or relax in one of their famous Silencio Rooms. Trained yoga instructors, like Nanga, tailor sessions to fit your needs.

"Modern society may make you want to rooooaaaarrr! Yoga, breathing, and meditation help calm that beast, make it purr, and cool it down for a catnap."

— Nanga

If Saharan luxury is what you're seeking, look no further than the Palm Hotel and Casino. This five-star hotel is centrally located and has rooms that boast amenities such as private pools, hibernation huts, and 360-degree views of the city.

The Palm is the official hotel of international singing sensation Gazelle.

"If I'm staying in Sahara Square, I'm at the Palm."

– Gazelle

ACCOMMODATING EVERY SIZE

You CAN see it all! With its great public transportation, it's easy to get around Zootopia.

Central Station and its trains are equipped for every size, so whether you're a giraffe, an elephant, or a rodent, you can catch your train here.

TO AND FROM BUNNYBURROW:
RABBIT TRANSIT

Getting to and from Bunnyburrow has never been easier, thanks to Rabbit Transit. With upgraded seats, free wireless, and café cars on every train, you may feel you got to your destination *too* quickly.

Separate entrances to the subway keep animals of every size safely on the move.

The metro runs through Zootopia and stops in each district—it couldn't be easier. Pick up a free map in Central Station or download the Metro app.

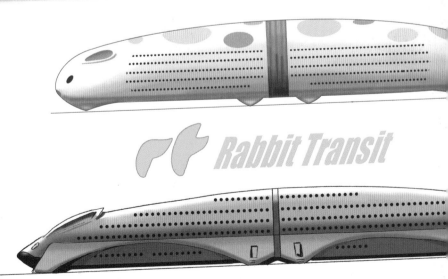

Rabbit Transit

Traveling within the city of Zootopia is easy. Mammals use a variety of ways to get around town. Some drive their own car or motorcycle, and many use public transportation or taxis. HerdShare, a citywide carpooling program, is also a great way to lumber where you need to go.

Because Zootopia is considered one of the top walking cities in the world, many citizens choose to get around the old-fashioned way—by hoof and paw.

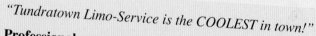

ZOOTOPIANS TO WATCH

Everyone knows that what really makes a city tick are the animals that live there. Zootopians like to say, "It's a jungle out there, but in Zootopia, anyone can be anything." Animals come from across the globe to make their dreams come true in this city of opportunity.

Gazelle is a household name throughout Zootopia. This hip-shaking pop singer, songwriter, vocalist, choreographer, and activist has been performing since she was a kid. Her first hit, "Try Everything," in which she belts out some of the highest notes known to mammals, was an instant #1 smash. It inspired a whole generation to believe that in Zootopia, you really can be anything.

"I'm inspired by everything in Zootopia. The beautiful animals . . . the peace and harmony . . . it just makes me want to siiiinnng."

-Gazelle

BUSINESS BIG SHOT:
MR. BIG

Self-made millionaire and Arctic shrew Mr. Big is one of the most successful business-mammals in Zootopia. This tycoon comes from humble beginnings; he was raised by his grandmother, who he remembers fondly. "Gram-mama taught me respect, determination, and above all else, the importance of family. She was the whole cannoli," Mr. Big says with a smile.

Mr. Big started small with a few tuxedo rental shops in Little Rodentia but quickly clawed his way to the top. Today he owns businesses across Zootopia. One of his most profitable is Tundratown Limo-Service.

Mr. Big lives in Tundratown with his soon-to-be-wed daughter, Fru Fru. "She's the light of my life. When she's happy, I'm happy. When she's unhappy . . . I do what I have to do."

A Zootopia-sized Dream: Officer Judy Hopps

As a young bunny growing up in Bunnyburrow, Judy dreamed of making a difference in the world. Though farming runs in the family—Hopps Family Farm is a popular staple in Bunnyburrow—Judy didn't want to be a farmer.

Officer Hopps is the first rabbit to graduate from the Zootopia Police Academy. And she already has a job with the Zootopia Police Department. "I can't wait to help keep the animals of Zootopia safe. I couldn't be more excited."

We asked Officer Hopps for her advice for anyone looking to make it in the big city. "Dream big. And don't let anyone tell you that you can't be what you want to be. Remember, in Zootopia, anyone can be anything." Spoken like a true Zootopian!

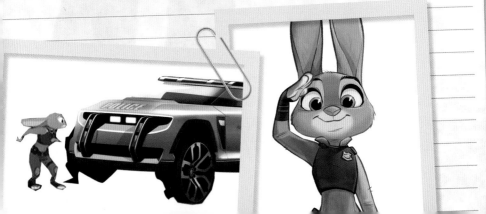

MEET THE MAYOR: LEODORE LIONHEART

A great city needs a great mayor. Leodore Lionheart is finishing his fourth year in office, and recent polls suggest he's on track to win reelection. Mayor Lionheart has implemented new programs, including the Mammal Inclusion Initiative, which he credits with producing the first rabbit police officer.

When asked what his priorities are, Lionheart says, "My number one concern is to keep Zootopia safe. If I do that, I will be reelected, and isn't that really what it's all about?"

Assistant Mayor:
Dawn Bellwether

Dawn Bellwether assists Mayor Lionheart with day-to-day tasks like scheduling meetings, fielding phone calls, and making sure the mayor has everything he needs to run the city. "Mayor Lionheart really appreciates all I do for him."

FOX ON THE STREETS:
NICK WILDE

Keep your eyes open as you stroll through Zootopia and chances are, you'll spot Nick Wilde. This lively fox has been working since he was twelve years old. He's always on the move. "I know everyone," he says, "and eight point five out of ten Zootopians know me."

We caught up with Nick and asked him a few questions.

OZH: What does it mean to be a Zootopian?

NW: It means living in the greatest city in the world. And that means great opportunity.

OZH: Describe a typical day in the life of Nick Wilde.

NW: If I did that, you'd know where to find me. But seriously, in a city like Zootopia, there are no typical days. Each one is better than the one before it.

KEEPING ZOOTOPIA HEALTHY:
DR. BADGER

Dr. Badger has been practicing medicine in Zootopia for years. She is known as one of the best doctors in the world, and has a long list of celebrity patients—including Mayor Lionheart. Dr. Badger works long hours, but we managed to get her on the phone during a break.

"Being a doctor requires a lifetime commitment. I work tirelessly toward a healthier community—all hours of the day and night. You know, those nocturnal mammals—they don't wait to call you in the morning if they have an issue. *(laughs)* But even I make time for myself every now and again. I tell all my patients. It's important."

BEST OF THE BEST:
DINING

One of the incredible things about Zootopia is its diversity, but it's not only the variety of animals that make it diverse—it's the variety of food. Whether you're a grazer or a gorger, an herbivore, an insectivore, or an omnivore, dining in Zootopia will satisfy.

The tuna tartar is incredible, and no one will bat an eye if you eat with your paws in the low-key atmosphere.

Dive in Thursday nights for their famous all-you-can-eat buffet!

Best Seafood:
Halibuts in Tundratown

If you're looking for a big ice cream sundae, it doesn't get any bigger—or better—than the jumbo sundae at Jumbeaux's Café. The chocolate peanut super sundae is award winning!

Best Sundae:
Jumbeaux's Café

Travel Tip:
Keep an eye on their app notifications for secret menu options!

Best Chopped Salad:
The Dunes

The chopped salad at the Dunes is always fresh and delicious. Swing by for lunch or dinner, and be sure to order the Armadillo Palmer for a cool, sweet, and tart drink!

Best Borscht:
Kozlov's Palace

The borscht at Kozlov's Palace is unbeatable. Enjoy a bowl at the Palace, and then buy a few jars to take home for a taste of the tundra anytime.

Best Fruit Smoothies:
The Tiki Hut

The Tiki Hut on Tujunga mixes up 137 different smoothie combinations. Try the pineapple strawberry cedar dream with a ginseng maggot boost and you'll zip through your day.

Happy Hour specials run from 3 to 5 p.m. and offer discounted prices on all super-sized smoothies!

Best Fries:
Wild Times

    Family amusement park Wild Times,
downtown on the pier, has plenty going on,
but one unexpected treat is the chili cheese
fries. The boardwalk fry stand is right by
the entrance to the park. Optional toppings
range from sautéed locusts and beetle bits
to live millipedes and grubs. Just like it
says on the rustic paper wrap they come in:
"Gooey, salty deliciousness."

BEST OF THE BEST:
NIGHTLIFE

Much of Zootopia lights up at night, when Zootopians who work all day can finally play. Check out these hot spots for nocturnal fun.

Best Shows:
Zootennial Stadium

This spectacular venue has stadium seating for 85,000 and hosts some of the most fur-raising shows in the world.

Check the schedule for special events that offer seating on the Prance Floor!

Best Amusement Park:
Wild Times

Scream therapy has never been more fun! Get your ya-yas out on stomach-flipping rides like Joy Ride, Cheetah Run, and the famous Roar-a-Coaster. Wild Times is family friendly and has plenty for the little ones. Try the carousel, bumper cars, or boardwalk games like Fetch the Stick and Log Roll.

Best Parade:
Rage 'n' Rave Parade

If you're lucky enough to catch the Rage 'n' Rave parade, it's a sight you'll never forget. Fire, glow sticks, and millions of twinkling lights light up the night as floats spin, glide, and swirl through downtown. The parade also features dancers, acrobats, and celebrity performers.

LOCAL FAVE:
THE NATURAL HISTORY MUSEUM

Travel back in time as you explore millions of prehistoric skeletons, artifacts, and fossils at the Natural History Museum.

Meet the Curator:
Dr. Zander Orshack

Dr. Orshack has been working at the Natural History Museum for the past twelve years. We visited with him in his downtown office and asked him a few questions.

OZH: What is it like to work at the world-famous Natural History Museum?

Dr. O: It's a thrill ride—like the fastest roller coaster at Wild Times, only it never stops! Seriously, I love my job. I get to work in this amazing place surrounded by mysteries, priceless artifacts, and ancient beasts. . . . I get to piece together the past—like a puzzle. And on coffee breaks, I look around and try to figure out which beasts I'm related to. *(laughs)* Is that you, Great-Great-Great-Uncle Equus? *(laughs)* Your skull—it's like I'm looking into an X-ray-powered mirror.

OZH: What's your favorite exhibit?

Dr. O: Ancient Giants. I adore the woolly mammoth. Its massive size is simply staggering.

OZH: Any other museum must-sees?

Dr. O: Mammal Mummies. It's so mysterious—examining them and imagining what their lives were like. King Mutt is my favorite because of all the folklore about the mummy being cursed. You can learn all about it at the museum.

OZH: What do you do when you're not working?

Dr. O: I play the flute in the Jazzy Z's, a jazz band. We perform at the Barnyard. Hoof it over on Wednesday nights and check us out sometime.

LOCAL FAVE:
FLORA

Zootopia's native plant species are as varied as its climates. Visitors come from all over to walk around and take in (and by "take in" we mean "eat") the glorious flora of Zootopia, from the Rainforest District's lush gardens to Sahara Square's unique cacti.

Palm Trees

Palm trees are found throughout Sahara Square, the Rainforest District, and downtown. Several different kinds of palms grow in Zootopia, some of which have fruit.

Tropical Plants and Flowers

Tropical plants and flowers just love the warm, misty air of the Rainforest District. Their abundance is a treat for the eyes and the stomach—sample any that look tasty to you.

LOCAL FAVE:
OTTERTON'S FLOWER SHOP

Otterton's Flower Shop has a wide variety of plants, bulbs, and cut flowers. Whether you want beautiful and exotic or delicious and crunchy, Otterton's has what you need.

Otterton's arrangements are perfect for weddings, birthdays, anniversaries, proms, and cat mitzvahs.

"The Old Goat arrangement I received from Otterton's for my ninety-second birthday was beautiful and delicious. It even came in an edible vase!"

— Mabel

TOP TEN WAYS TO ACT LIKE A NATIVE

When in Zootopia you:

1. Know that Cliffside Asylum is NOT the name of a local band.
2. Pronounce Tujunga like "Tuh-hunga."
3. Pronounce Zoosten like "Zow-sten."
4. Avoid parking in areas with bunny meter maids.
5. Join Gazelle onstage in the Gazelle app.
6. Celebrity watch at the Palm.
7. Let the good times roll at Wild Times.
8. Form a kickline anytime you hear Jerry Vole's "Zootopia, Zootopia."
9. Always tell the truth to Mr. Big.
10. Remember the mantra: "In Zootopia, anyone can be anything."

AD PAGES

BE A FRIEND
WITHOUT A DOUBT.
BE A JUNIOR
RANGER SCOUT.

Scouts earn badges that they can wear with pride!

IT'S NOT JUST GOOD . . .
IT'S REAL GOOD.

Gideon Grey's Real Good Baked Stuff . . .
made with Hopps Family Farm produce.

"In addition to my pies, try my new kickin' cayenne cakes!"

"It's like a thousand burrs on your tongue!"

CLASSIFIEDS

HELP WANTED

Fast-talking receptionist needed in sloth law office.

Now hiring dormouse for historic hotel in Little Rodentia.

Got a license? See in the dark? Drive a cab! Oryx Taxi Company needs drivers like YOU.

GIGS

Do you snarl like a hyena and growl like a bear? The Howling Jackals are seeking a new singer. Call Spider.

Paw models needed for Sunday shoot. Send pictures to Buck Modeling Agency.

Looking for babysitter. Must have experience with biters. Text Mrs. Nibbles.

Make money at home in your underwear selling insurance! No experience necessary! Call Beatrix.

FOR SALE

Lose your paunch and buy my authentic Pot-Bellied Treadmill. Text Peter Oinkawitz.

Like-new Little Kitty playhouse with scratching post and tunnel. Perfect for keeping young felines active and out of your fur! Message: momof36.

Used synthesizer. Gnaw marks on a few keys but works fine. Good price. Contact Jenny.

9p iPaw, still in mint condition. Message Paula.

Three tix to Jerry Vole at the Canyon Club Saturday night. Call Raul.

ROOMS/REAL ESTATE

Small acrobatic shrew seeks spacious apartment in Little Rodentia. Call Alexis.

Room for rent in party pad, Tundratown adjacent. Text Tony.

Traveling musician needs room for month of May in Sahara Square. Can't pay but will cook. Possibly clean. Message: Room4Food

---

Vintage mouse pad for sale in Little Rodentia.

SERVICES OFFERED

Organized gopher available for pack rats. I do closets, kitchens, offices, and more! Call Carla.

Mangy? Grooming done in the comfort of your home. I come to you! Catcutshair.com.

PERSONALS

If you were buying a quart of milk at Cheese 'n' Crackers last night and smiled at me, I love you.

To the skunk who dented my car without leaving a note yesterday: you stink.

Cougar seeks young foodie who loves long strolls on the beach and salsa dancing.

If you're looking for a construction worker with a heart of gold, find me at Sammy's Sammies at noon.

Itchy? Me too! Scratch exchange Wednesdays at noon in Center Park by the pond.

MY ZOOTOPIA
TRAVEL JOURNAL

Ready to plan your trip to Zootopia?
These journal pages will help you get
organized so you can make the most of your
time in this great city.

My Must-See Attractions:

Restaurants to Try:

Interesting Boutiques and Shops:

Tours I Want to Take:

Locals I'd Love to Meet: